Retold by
Tony Mitton

Illustrated by
Mike Redman

CHARLES DICKENS

A Christmas Carol

ORCHARD

To Sue Buswell, with thanks – T.M.

For Mum, Dad, Tom and Soph – M.R.

ORCHARD BOOKS
First published in Great Britain in 2018 by The Watts Publishing Group
2 4 6 8 10 9 7 5 3 1

Text © Tony Mitton 2018
Illustrations © Mike Redman 2018

The moral rights of the author and illustrator have been asserted.
All rights reserved. A CIP catalogue record for this book is
available from the British Library.

ISBN 978 1 40835 167 3

Printed and bound in China

MIX
Paper from
responsible sources
FSC® C104740
FSC
www.fsc.org

Orchard Books, an imprint of Hachette Children's Group
Part of The Watts Publishing Group Limited
Carmelite House, 50 Victoria Embankment
London EC4Y 0DZ

An Hachette UK Company
www.hachette.co.uk

www.hachettechildrens.co.uk

In London Town there lived a man.
His fortune, it was huge.
But he was mean and miserly,
old Ebenezer Scrooge.

Our story starts on Christmas Eve
as day was dying down.
Old Scrooge sat checking his accounts,
as ever, with a frown.

His clerk, Bob Cratchit, sat nearby,
scratching with his quill.
From time to time he rubbed his hands
to warm them from the chill.

For Scrooge, being mean and miserly,
would keep his chamber cold.
The way he measured out the coal
you'd think that it were gold.

The office clock chimed closing time.
Bob Cratchit gave a cough.
"Tomorrow's Christmas Day, sir.
So may I take it off?"

Scrooge gave Bob a narrow look.
"A day off? If you must.
But I won't pay you for that day."
His voice was dry as dust.

Poor Cratchit nodded nervously.

"Sir, Merry Christmas, then . . ."

"Christmas? Humbug!" Scrooge replied.

"A feast for foolish men."

Scrooge closed up his office.
He went back to his room.
He ate his bowl of lonely gruel,
surrounded by the gloom.

But then the mournful ghost appeared
of Marley, his dead friend.
"I warn you, Scrooge, to mend your ways,
before you meet your end."

Scrooge merely muttered, "Humbug!
You're just a puff of smoke.
Don't talk to me of kindness . . .
and Christmas cheer's a joke!"

He changed into his nightgown
and tucked himself in bed.
And as he blew his candle out,
"Christmas? Bah!" he said.

But as the darkness gathered,
a figure with white hair
came shining straight towards him.
Scrooge murmured, "Who goes there?"

"I am the Ghost of Christmas Past.
And you must come with me.
For I have things to show you.
Things that you must see."

They floated through the chilly air
till Scrooge let out a groan.
He saw his boyhood self, so sad,
sitting quite alone.

The other boys had all gone home
to family Christmas cheer,
leaving poor young Scrooge at school,
so silent, cold and drear.

And then he saw his young-man self,
rejecting, hour by hour,
the chance of love and happiness
to gain more wealth and power.

"Oh, Ghost," the miser murmured,
"These memories bring me pain.
I pray you leave them in the past.
Oh, take me home again."

Scrooge felt himself transported
to such a startling scene!
His room was full of festive fare
and a jolly giant in green!

"I am the Ghost of Christmas Present,
come to show you more.
I bring you Christmas here and now,
for folk both rich and poor."

They flew through many a bustling street,
where cheerful people shopped.
They came upon Bob Cratchit's house,
and there the giant stopped.

Although the scene was bare and poor
it shone with care and love.
Scrooge felt a tug upon his heart
while gazing from above.

Bob Cratchit's crippled son was there,
So pallid, frail and ill.
"Will Tiny Tim recover?"
Scrooge whispered –
"Say he will . . ."

The giant, silent, flew him on
to view the working poor
who grimly toiled by night and day
to swell the rich folks' store.

Scrooge witnessed how they laboured.
They had no choice. They must.
They worked their bitter lives away
to earn a meagre crust.

Then as the vision faded,
Scrooge found himself in bed.
A hooded shape approached him
which filled his heart with dread.

"The Ghost of Christmas Future,"
within his mind he heard.
The silent spirit took him
with neither look nor word.

They floated to Bob Cratchit's house
where sorrow filled the air.
For Tiny Tim lay dying –
a sight Scrooge could not bear.

The silent spirit led him on
to a corpse beneath a veil.
"Oh, whose is this, cruel spectre?"
Scrooge trembled and grew pale.

The spirit told him nothing,
but led poor Scrooge away
to a drear, deserted graveyard
where a lone and plain grave lay.

And there upon the gravestone
Scrooge saw his name shown clear.
"I beg you, Spirit, tell me,
does my own death draw near . . . ?"

The ghost stayed still and silent
as light began to rise.
It merged into his bedpost
before his very eyes.

"Then was this real, or just a dream?
Who cares? For I'm still here!
I have a chance to make amends
and spread some Christmas Cheer!"

Scrooge ran to pull the window up.
A boy was passing by.
"Say, what's today?" he shouted out.
The boy gave this reply:

"Why, Christmas Day, of course, sir."
Said Scrooge, "I'm not too late
to put some Christmas turkey
on poor Bob Cratchit's plate."

He paid the boy a shilling
to take a turkey there.
And then he went to buy some gifts
for the Cratchits all to share.

And later when he called on them
to spread some Christmas fun,
Tiny Tim cried heartily,
"God bless us, everyone!"

Then as they sat to dinner
Scrooge made a Christmas vow
to be a better boss to Bob
and pay him well from now.

But more than that, he'd use his wealth
to help the sick and poor.
For what's the point of money
that gathers dust in store?

And that's how Scrooge, the Miser,
was changed to Scrooge, the Man,
who keeps as kind a Christmas
as any person can.

So let us do like dear old Scrooge
as Christmas time draws near —
and fill the world with peace and love,
with kindness and good cheer!